ABBY'S SEARCH FOR COOPER

by

Paula Burns

Illustrated by

Haylea Young

Abby's Search For Cooper

Published by
NORTH COUNTRY BOOKS, INC.
PUBLISHER—DISTRIBUTOR
311 Turner Street
Utica, New York 13501

Printed in Hong Kong

For Carla, Erin and Jon, my treasures in this life.

Thank you to Haylea's Christopher and Brittany,

our "awesome" little critics.

Special love and appreciation to Jerry, whose

encouragement taught Abby and me never to give up.

This book is dedicated
to the memory of my father,
Carl Ennis,
a beloved artist who truly loved
all creatures great and small.

I am Abby,

a gentle golden retriever,

and from the time I was a

light yellow pup,

I have been visiting a wonderful

magical place called

Cooperstown

It is a special town where the game of baseball was born.

Since my puppy days I have gone
there to fish with my young
master Jonathan and his Mom and Dad.

Jonathan's Mom used to say, "Abby you are such
a beautiful golden. Someday you may meet a handsome
golden retriever in this town. Wouldn't it be great if he were
named Cooper, since we all love Cooperstown so much."

What great times my family and I have spent
in Cooperstown. We have often gone to Council Rock,
a famous meeting place of the Indians long ago.

It was there by the quiet lake that Jonathan learned
to fish and I met a little friend, we called Toadie.
What fun we had darting in and out of the water.
But I didn't see any handsome golden retrievers.

When Jonathan tired of fishing we would walk to
another part of the lake where we found a lovely
park with ducks and birds to watch. I especially
enjoyed tumbling and playing on the grass as
the ducks and geese strutted about.

In this park there is a splendid statue of
an Indian hunter and his dog. The
sculpture looks so real—what loyal companions
the Indian and his dog must have been.

INDIAN
HUNTER AND
HIS DOG.

Next up to Main Street we would go while
Jonathan visited the baseball card shops.

Once Jonathan's Mom took a picture of us by another statue
called "The Sandlot Kid." This famous boy and his
baseball bat are located near Doubleday Field.
I loved to watch all the visitors hurrying by to
see the sights at the museums. Some even stopped
to tell me how pretty I was.

As I grew I wondered if my
"Cooper" would think I was pretty too.

One of the very best treats in Cooperstown is the bakery with its many pies, cakes and cookies. We always stop for a gingerbread boy for Jonathan and one for me too.

Yes, we have had many happy times at Cooperstown.
I am not a little puppy any more. I am taller and
my fur has gotten redder. The Mom said that it
looked as if I had grown pants. One day while
walking back toward the lake we stopped at a house
with a small yard to admire nine golden retriever puppies
and their proud mother named Morgan. I wondered
if she happened to know the friend I had been searching for.

I was just about to give up looking for my golden.
Then, one day while we were fishing at Council Rock,
I saw a magnificent dog bounding toward us from a
huge house. Imagine my surprise when I heard
a voice call out, "Come back, Cooper."

Well, Jonathan's Mom has said that life doesn't always
turn out as you expect it. Cooper is not a golden retriever,
but he is a very handsome yellow Labrador. We were
happy to meet each other and our families were happy to meet.
Now we all have picnics together at Council Rock.
Sometimes we stroll uptown for an ice cream cone.
Cooper has introduced me to Sandy, another yellow Lab,
who naps at the bait shop each day.

Once we all walked by the Baseball Hall of Fame
and they were filming a movie about a women's
softball team from years ago. Cooper and I
wished we could be in that movie.

One day I knew something really special was going to happen
in Cooperstown. There was excitement in the air and the
town was even more crowded with people than usual.
I found out that every summer two very important baseball
teams arrive to play each other in a thrilling game.
I could tell my family was happy to be going, but I was sad
when I learned that even good dogs were not allowed.

Well, I wasn't unhappy for long because I spent that day at Cooper's house with Cooper and his family. They have a friendly cat called Ginger Kitty. She likes to arch her back, stretching her seven-toed paws and to touch her whiskers to my nose.

I am looking forward to many happy adventures with Cooper. He didn't turn out to be a golden retriever like me, but he is my friend and he is great!